Gods, Teens, and Inbetweens

Colin Davidson

Published by Travis Cramer, 2024.

This is a work of fiction. Similarities to real people, places, or events are entirely coincidental.

GODS, TEENS, AND INBETWEENS

First edition. October 23, 2024.

Written by Colin Davidson.

Table of Contents

This book is dedicated to the following people: Travis Cramer, a good friend and very helpful editor.

My Moldy Chicken sandwich that never made it out of the lunch box. RIP.

And finally to all short and tall people alike.

Whirls of noise collide,

Unraveled threads pull the world,

Order lost in time.

A haiku by Travis Cramer

By: Collin Davidson
Gods, Teens, and
In-betweens

FOREWORD BY TRAVIS CRAMER

So, when my friend, Colin Davidson, told me that he wanted to write a fanfiction based off of my book series, I was like, 'okay, sure, I'm cool with that. Just give me some credit, given that it was my book series that started it.' Well, he didn't give me any credit, so...

Okay, I'm kidding – he gave me as much credit as I deserved, which, given how completely different this book is from my book series, honestly isn't much. As the author himself said, "If you change the character's names, the book has nothing to do with your book series." Frankly, I'm inclined to agree with him...Greek gods, electrocuted squirrels...what a mess.

Side note: You know what's wild...after I wrote this forward...he changed all the character names. So I guess it has nothing to do with the book series. Is even a fanfic anymore? Man, I don't know...anyway, ignore this side note and keep reading.

A mess in a good way, of course. His book is at times chaotic, at times...possibly disturbing (okay, I'm kidding), but all in all, it's hilarious. It's the kind of book that you read on an airplane and annoy every other passenger by laughing really loudly every few seconds.

If you're looking for a book that you want to curl up and read next to the fireplace (do they still have those) or a book that you want to read under the covers instead of going to bed...you should keep looking. (May I suggest the Misadventure and Mystery book series? Yes, shameless plug,

I know, I know.) This isn't that kind of book. It's not cozy and it's not relaxing...it's jampacked with action, twists, and of course, humor!!

All in all, I can give my full support for my friend in writing this book. Who knows...maybe he'll go on to be even more successful then me...anything can happen! (Although, if he starts to make millions of dollars, I might demand a cut...better watch out.) You won't be disappointed when you read this book, so, grab yourself some Pop-Rocks (seems fitting)...maybe put on the theme for Mission Impossible and get lost in a good book. You know you want to! The book cover is just begging you. (Oh and did I mention that he drew that cover himself. No? Well, now you know!)

-Travis Cramer

PROLOGUE:

"Carlos will rot in a compost bin, steaming hot, in my compost bin. Hee...hee...hee..." a skinny old man said to himself. He wore an odd white robe that failed to cover his scarred and bony chest. "Steal the power of the great Zeus! I think not! I still got it in me," he continued talking to himself.

CHAPTER 1

A Completely Different Place

"Hey yo, Grids! What up, bro—I mean, babe?" Alex, Ingrid's gangster boyfriend, said. "So, babe, I was wondering if we could reschedule our date tonight? Curty and Kev wanna go surfing, and I kinda said that I would go, so like, ya know..."

Ingrid gave him an unamused stare. "But this was the rescheduled date from last week, and you have a habit of rescheduling." She paused, trying to logically deduce whether the date would ever happen. "Fine, you can go, but I fail to see why you want to surf; it seems like an unnecessarily silly form of transportation."

"Thanks, babe!" Alex said, getting ready to leave. "But surfing isn't for transportation, it's for the vibes." He was about to leave when Ingrid realized she had to add some restrictions, as Alex could be wild at times.

"Wait," she said, eyeing him. "You can only go if you promise not to drink... or try to get a one-day girlfriend. If you do, I'm breaking up with you," she said straightforwardly. She had learned to speak her mind when telling Alex what not to do.

"Of course, babe, you got it," he said as if he would never consider doing anything foolish. In reality, he probably was going to wake up with a massive headache the next morning.

CHAPTER ii
Another Completely Different Place

"Haa-haa-haa...How you like me nowwwww?" Andrew said as he grooved on the sidewalk. He started doing the moonwalk, then transitioned to fluid motions with his arms, making him look like he didn't have bones or something of the sort. "Hey City! Where is Carlos? I didn't see him anywhere in class," he said to a female figure staring at something on the sidewalk.

"Woah, dude! You look like you're a seagull. What? How are you doing that?" Felicity asked, looking down at a stuffed animal seagull lying on the ground. "I'm tired. What is it those doctors gave me again?" Andrew grabbed her shoulder and shook her.

"Felicity, that's not me," he said, referencing the cute little puff of a heinous flying demon of the sea. She looked up at him. "Now, come on. Are you sure you took the right amount of pain meds?" Andrew asked, helping her up. He tried to help her walk to his car, which was a relatively short distance away.

"I guesstimated... I think I might need to take some more... 'cause my head feels funky," Felicity said, sitting down on the sidewalk and looking around aimlessly. Andrew just put his hand on his head, regretting offering to drive her to college and back.

Felicity took a pill bottle out of her pocket and went to open it. Andrew grabbed her hand, saying, "Uhh, I think you've had enough of those." He took the bottle and stored it in his backpack. Upon seeing her pills taken, Felicity halfheartedly reached for the bottle but quickly decided to lie down on the grass instead.

"Andrew, why don't we always lie on the grass? It's so nice and soft. Come on, try it..." She lay there contentedly, but Andrew tried to rouse her back to her feet.

"Andrew, leave me alone. Stop pulling my arm," she complained, but he continued anyway.

"Felicity, we need to get going! You can't just lie on the grass in the middle of campus. Come on, get up!" He managed to get her to stand and walk a little.

"This is boring. I don't want to walk anymore. It hurts my legs!" she said, then almost completely stopped holding up her weight, though her arms were wrapped around his neck. Andrew wobbled a bit from her sudden limpness, but he kept his arm around her, which at least helped him carry her tired body. Upon realizing she was only being dragged along, Felicity began walking again, realizing he wasn't going to stop.

"I'm tired... I have to go pee... Can we take a break?" she asked, looking up at Andrew.

"No, you're acting like a child. Will you please just keep walking?" he said, motioning forward in frustration. Felicity lazily rolled her eyes, continuing to lean on him as they walked. "Look, the car's right there," he said, pointing at his somewhat old and beat-up car.

"You're a butt!" Felicity said dozily. "I don't like you anymore... No, that's not true. You're okay," she said, then kissed him on the cheek. There wasn't much he could do in response, except wish she'd start acting more normal; it felt weird getting kissed on the cheek by one of his friend's girlfriends.

"Alright, now you can sit in here," he said, trying to get her situated in the passenger seat of his car. Once she was settled, he walked around to the other side. As he did, she leaned over and started pressing the horn.

"Felicity! Stop pressing that, please!"

"I'm sorry..." Felicity said, looking at him suspiciously as he sat in the driver's seat.

She had stopped the honking but now leaned over to kiss him on the cheek. "Uh, no thank you," Andrew said, pushing her back to her seat as she attempted to lean over as far as humanly possible.

Felicity sat back in her seat. "I'm breaking up with Derek," she said, slouching now. Proper posture wasn't exactly on her mind. "He's a loser... Can I be your girlfriend? No, you don't want me. I'm not pretty enough. But I don't even like Derek..." She continued, but her speech devolved into more unintelligible rambling.

Andrew—now driving—tried to focus on the road through the constant onslaught of her ramblings but realized he really wasn't, as he'd missed his turn.

"Where are we going again? Whose car did we steal?" Felicity tapped the radio and grabbed a knob.

"We didn't steal anyone's car. Now, can you please stop messing with the radio?" Andrew swatted her hand away as she flipped through stations. Finally, he pulled into a gas station since his car was running low on fuel.

"That wasn't very nice," Felicity complained. "Why'd you hit me? You shouldn't hit people. And... and... I'm tired..." She folded her arms and leaned back. Andrew shut off the car and got out to pump gas.

'What pain meds did she take...how many?' Andrew thought to himself. He paid for the gas, got back into the car, and drove toward the campus. He didn't think it was wise to leave Felicity by herself in her current state. He also wasn't sure how much he was supposed to hang around in her room, but it seemed like the only option.

Pulling into the parking lot, he parked and got out of the car. They were in a co-ed dorm hall, so everyone stayed in the same general area, meaning they lived quite close to each other. "Come on, let's get you up to your room," Andrew said, helping her out of the car. They got a few odd stares and giggles from the passersby as he helped her into her room.

Setting her things down on the floor, Andrew helped Felicity onto the bed before sitting on a chair at her desk, causing a few squeaks.

"Andrew," she said, snuggling into her pillows and blankets. "Can you get me the flicker? I want to watch something."

"The what?" They both paused for a moment, each wondering if the other was mentally unwell—because physical insanity could also be a legitimate possibility. "What are you talking about? What's a flicker?" Andrew asked, positive Felicity wasn't thinking straight. (Reasonable, given her current state.)

"The flicker—you know, the thing that controls the TV," she said, staring at the ceiling. "Can you get me a Gatorade too? I think I have one... maybe."

"You mean the remote? Uhh, sure." He grabbed it and found her Gatorade in the fridge, then handed them both to her.

CHAPTER iii

A Different Place

"Hey, Duellona, can you help me kill this kid?" Zeus asked over the phone. "Actually, while we're at it, Athena might want somebody I know dead as well."

"Zeusy, you know I stopped doing that kind of thing a while ago. Killing random kids is a big 'no-no' nowadays. Besides, I'm not an assassin," a woman's voice responded over the phone. "And surprise, surprise, Athena is hacking our call."

"Hey, Athena!" Zeus yelled into the phone. "Do you want Fobee dead? I think it would be beneficial." He leaned back in his rocking chair and cracked his shoulder with one arm.

"Zeus, why are you in a robe, and why does this robe fail to cover your chest? Just... ewww. You do know that's out of style, right? It is not wise to so blatantly go against the cultural norm. But back to the topic: The name is pronounced Ingrid. And yes, I think it would be wise," Athena said in a very sophisticated, feminine voice.

"Wait, how can you see me? What, do you have spies again? You—you actually agree we should kill them? Whoopie!" Zeus said, first distressed, then excited.

"The cameras are very useful for spying. I no longer need living servants to do my bidding," Athena said. Zeus immediately put his thumb over his phone's camera.

"The security cameras are easy to look through as well," she added. Zeus became frantic once more.

"But I have security cameras everywhere—even in the bathrooms..." Zeus half-sobbed, running aimlessly to escape her watch until he slid under a rug.

"And I turned those off a while ago," Athena said carelessly. "They aren't a useful security feature, so I deemed them a waste of precious energy. Also, I can see the bump in the rug—that is, I can see you."

"You're a creep! I'm never inviting you to bingo night ever again," Zeus said, peeking out from under his rug.

"Nobody has ever gone to bingo night with you," Duellona noted, teaming up with Athena against Zeus. "Anyway, if we're gonna take out these kids, I want both of you there with me."

"But why do I have to be there?" Zeus whined in a childish tone of sorrow.

CHAPTER iv

A Completely Different Place: At the Beach with Alex, Ingrid's Boyfriend

"Kev, Curty, you guys made it! You know, I canceled my date with Grids tonight so I could make this, and I'm so glad I did! Is that spiked tea I see? Give me one of those!" Alex said, grabbing and gulping down a tea.

Three Hours Later:

Alex was lying on the beach, feeling a little woozy. His phone started ringing next to him, and he immediately answered it. "Hey, thi—thid—is Alex. What do yuh want?"

"Are you drunk?" came a sharp voice over the phone.

"Maybe, maybe not, but probably maybe... Wait, who'd dis? You're ruining the vibes, and I'mma trying to get tanned." He flopped his head to the other side to stop looking at the sun.

"This is Ingrid—your ex-girlfriend—seeing how you most likely tried to find another already... You sound drunk."

"I had to stay hydrated somehow, you know. Nobody brought water; guess they figured there was enough in the ocean. But salt water is so salty. So I wasn't g-gonna drink it, but thirst will kill yuh out here... so like, yeah." He rolled over in the sand.

"What is this, the 20th time you forgot to bring water? I'm not buying it—we're through," Ingrid responded angrily.

"Wait... you're not dumping me, are you? You can't dump me... I didn't do anything wrong! I only had a couple of sips, man—barely anything."

"Yes, I'm dumping you; go die in a hole!" Ingrid hung up the phone. Chin in hand, she rested it on a table.

"Please don't ever date someone with below-average IQ again, Ingrid," she told herself out loud. "So much for rescheduling the date!" she continued, slightly irritated but, in a way, glad because Alex could be very annoying sometimes. She took her phone off the table in front of her and called Felicity.

"Hey, Ingrid, it's me," Andrew said, answering the phone.

"Uhh, you're definitely not Felicity... Who is this? Andrew?" Ingrid asked, lifting her right eyebrow and laying back on her comfy couch. "What are you doing with Felicity? Oh, you offered to drive her or something, didn't you? Well, can I talk to her? Where are you?"

"At the moment, we're in her room, because... well, it's kind of a story. I think she took too many of her painkillers because she's been acting, umm, a little off," Andrew said, looking over at Felicity, who was blinking to stay awake while watching a love movie.

"Theodore, it can't be. We can never be together," said a female character.

"I can't live without you; I'd rather die than be alone."

"They can't tell us what to do our whole lives. We can run away and make a life for ourselves!" replied the character Theodore.

"This is awful. Who made this movie? These actors are terrible; they're such drama queens," Felicity complained. "Why are there flowers growing on a rock cliff in the middle of winter? They literally just taped fake flowers onto the stone." She turned off the movie and started looking for another.

"What did she take, and how many?" Ingrid asked. Andrew tried to read the name on the bottle but mumbled more gibberish than actual words.

"Okay, I'm gonna head over there," Ingrid said, getting off her couch.

"I thought you had a date tonight. We're honestly fine—you don't have to come. I mean, if you're going to miss your date, don't," Andrew said, trying not to sound cliché or all up in her business.

"No, I, uh... I sort of dumped him. But that's for the best. He wasn't what you'd call a great boyfriend—or friend, for that matter. Anyhow, I'm heading over, so I'll see you in five minutes."

"Ohh, uhh, okay. Bye," Andrew said before hanging up the phone. "Ingrid's coming over," he announced to the room. He was, to some degree, happy that Ingrid dumped Alex. They made a remarkably bad pair.

Felicity gave up on the TV and pushed her head back into her pillow. "Why's Grids coming over? I didn't invite her."

"Well, she just said she was. Nobody invited her. Besides, it would be nice to have some more company," Andrew said, leaning against the desk.

"Well, I guess I'm not good enough company, then," Felicity said, looking across the covers she was lying under. "You probably don't even want to be around me. I don't got a chance of... of..." She unintelligibly mumbled the rest, sounding very drowsy.

"Felicity, if I didn't want to be here, I wouldn't be. Actually, I'd probably still be here, but that's not the point. Now, can you please stop whatever this is?" Andrew said, done with Felicity's nonsensical ranting.

"Wow, somebody's rude... Can I have my phone?" Felicity asked, sitting up.

"Uhh, sure," Andrew said, handing her the phone. "But what do you want it for?" he asked.

"I'm just calling somebody, okay?" Felicity said lazily. "Stop being so nosy." Andrew sat down in his chair, trying to ignore what she said. Dealing with drugged-up Felicity was getting exhausting; he just wanted to go to sleep, even though it was probably only 5:30.

Felicity's phone made a little noise to signify it was calling, but it went to voicemail after a minute. Felicity groaned, irritated that her call wasn't answered, and decided to leave a voicemail. "I'm breaking up with you, Derek. It's just not working for me, so, yeah... Umm, it might seem sudden, but it's not. Uhh, this is Felicity... umm, have a nice day, and don't call back 'cause I'm, like, too tired to deal with you... bye now," she ended the message.

Andrew looked up from the desk, as he had been using his arms as a pillow. "Wait, who'd you just call?"

As soon as he finished speaking, there was a knock on the door. Ingrid opened it herself, as she didn't really care about being let in—in her mind, they already knew she was coming anyway.

"Nobody. I just broke up with Derek, that's all," Felicity said, noticing Ingrid walking into the little apartment. "Hey, In—Ing—Ingry—Ingrid-oh, whatcha doing?"

"Just Ingrid, thank you. As for my errand, I don't exactly have a clear one, but I thought it would be helpful not to leave you and Andrew alone," Ingrid cleared her throat. "As Andrew, no offense, doesn't know the first thing about medications or taking care of people."

"Wait, why do I need to be cared for? I feel fine..." Felicity half-argued, but she didn't seem like she was paying much attention to anything.

"Wait, what do you mean you broke up with him?" Andrew asked, going back to the previous conversation. "What did you say to him? How do you just break up with someone like that?" Andrew disregarded the apparently insulting comment from Ingrid, as Felicity gave him a bigger fish to fry.

Felicity: "I just left him a..." at the same time Ingrid: "I told him to..." pause...

Ingrid: "You broke up with Derek? What, I thought..."

Felicity: "You broke up with Alex? I didn't like him anyway, but..."

"Yeah, but why did you break up with Derek? He said he wanted to marry you eventually; that must have been hard for him to hear," Ingrid said, thinking about how Derek took it.

"No, I just left a voicemail... He said he wanted to marry me? Gross," Felicity said, shrugging her shoulders and chewing her lip.

"What?" Andrew practically yelled. "Felicity, you can't do that; you're gonna really hurt him."

"It was his fault he didn't answer the phone... I don't wanna talk about this," Felicity said, turning over in her bed. "I don't like you guys mad at me... I just... I just... I don't want to be... I wanna be your... whatever... just leave me alone." Her thoughts didn't come out how she thought them, and she felt like giving up.

"Andrew," Ingrid said, "I'll tell Derek what's going on. There's no point discussing this more with Felicity; she doesn't really seem all there at the moment."

"What do you mean all there? I'm all everywhere, wait, say what again?" Felicity looked about confused.

CHAPTER v

A place that is completely different:

Carlos, a short Hispanic fellow, decided it was time to test his electrical contraption on a living subject. This subject was sitting on the ground eating a nut—it was Murphy the squirrel. The idea behind the weapon was very confusing and, in the end, seemed to make no sense, but he had gotten his weapon to be able to shoot a small dart-shaped device that would shock anything that was within about a foot and a half of it.

He shot, and Murphy looked up when he heard "Cli-clink-pfhh," and his eyes looked at the oncoming dart. It hit him square in the head and Murphy fell over, kicking. Carlos wasn't sure if it was because of the electric shock or the hit to the head. He didn't intend to kill Murphy; he only gave the dart a bit of charge, so it would at most knock Murph unconscious.

Carlos grabbed the slack body of Murphy and his dart. It had a rounded tip, so it should have just given him a bad headache. Murphy's body tensed up, and his mouth opened, showing big blunt yellow teeth, which instantly went to bite the hand of his captor. Carlos freaked out and chucked Murphy up in the air. Luckily for Murphy, he flew into a tree and was able to stop himself before hitting the ground.

Murphy watched with an evil stare as Carlos left the "scene of the crime." Carlos murmured to himself, "Well, that test was inconclusive."

And Murphy schemed against Carlos, looking for a way he could get revenge.

Sweet revenge...

CHAPTER vi

Once again, a different place:

"Well, why are we at this school, Duellona? This isn't their college; this is a child's school," Zeus asked, as they walked up to a large school.

"Euphrosyne goes to school here," Athena said, in a very uplifting, pleasant voice.

"Do you have to answer questions even when they aren't directed towards you?" Duellona asked, rolling her eyes. "And Zeus, can you please change into something more modern? You stick out like a sore thumb in a whipped cream forest."

"No, everyone just doesn't want to admit that I dress normally because it proves that they dress oddly," Zeus profoundly proclaimed. "And why do we need her? I've never liked her. She's always giggling and smiley, and it's unnatural. She really gives me the creeps!"

"Joy seems unnatural for a miserable person," Athena reflected. "We do not need—" Duellona loudly interrupted Athena.

"What did I say about answering for me? Zeus, we need her as we need you. We don't, but it's nice to do something together again," Duellona actually sounded relatively sweet at the end, saying "together again."

"So, you made me miss bingo night because you wanted to hang out, but why couldn't we hang out playing bingo?" Zeus asked, confused.

"Because I prefer things that require more action and planning, not hoping you win a game based on luck," Duellona said. At this point, they were standing and talking, no longer walking towards the school.

A little 7- or 8-year-old-looking girl came running up to them. She was wearing a simple dress. "Duellona, Zeus, Athena! I'm so happy to see you, it's been so long!" She started hugging each of them, but she was much shorter. She had a bright smile and was almost explosive with joy as her little dress spun around her when she moved.

"We're gonna take out some college students, want to come?" Duellona asked, in such a way it almost made it sound like a normal pastime.

"Of course I want to go! Are we going now, or should I get my knife later?" Euphrosyne asked, then perked up a little more. "Ohh, wait, I got my knife on me; I'm all ready to go! It'll make me so happy finally dealing with Felicity!"

"Who's Felicity?" Zeus asked as Euphrosyne pulled out a Kukri. "Umm, don't you...that looks dangerous."

"How else would we dispatch them?" Euphrosyne asked, giggling. "I always liked the old way the best!" She sounded oddly cheery saying this disturbing thing.

"True, to some extent, although there are some ways that would be more discrete and cause less of a disturbance," Athena said, not seeming to be affected by the strange amount of joy Euphrosyne had from the idea of murder. "Zeus, you seem troubled by her joy. You must know Euphrosyne will always be happy in whatever she does—it is her gift—her nature. Even if it seems strange to you, she cannot help it."

"Yeah," Zeus said, raising his right eyebrow, "It does seem strange to me because it is. Maybe she should be happy about something else, like bingo night, not murdering people. It's creepy."

"Will you shut up, Zeus! Nobody wants to hear about bingo night, and your thoughts on her being happy. Just leave her alone. Besides, you're being a hypocrite. You were happy when we said we'd do this," Duellona said.

"Yeah, but why does she want to kill that girl Felicity? Probably because she's too happy, so Euphrosyne is jealous," Zeus argued.

"If we're getting the old gang back together, can we dress like we used to? I think we looked awesome," Euphrosyne asked. She would completely block things out if they would make her unhappy if she thought too much about them. Normally it was things like criticism, or if a friend died, that she blocked out.

"I do not think it would be wise to dress so flagrantly as we used to. Our old dress is now greatly different from any modern form of clothing found in North Carolina," Athena advised, as advising was one of her favorite hobbies.

"Heck with it..." Duellona said. "Why do we care if people look at us weird? They'll probably just assume we're actors or something anyway."

They soon were walking out of a gas station bathroom dressed elegantly in long robes, jewelry, and such, varying between each of them. Euphrosyne was taller and looked like she was 16, and the kukri fit her size better than before. Her clothing was closer to a modern dress than Athena's or Duellona's. Zeus didn't change, as he was already in the same type of robe he had always worn.

You get the idea of what this means by now:

"Hey, what are you doing here, Talia?" Andrew asked, opening up the door to Felicity's room for her, as she had knocked.

"Ingrid texted me that 'City' wasn't feeling good, so I figured I might as well come over," Talia said, shrugging her shoulders. Andrew let her in, and a minute later they heard another knock; Andrew opened up the door again.

"What's wrong with Felicity? Ingrid wasn't very clear," Carlos asked, then walked into the room that was now pretty full with them all in it.

"I just took too many pills, I don't know why all y'all are acting crazy 'cause I'm fine!" Felicity said, swinging her head a bit as she elongated some words. "What are we gonna do now that everyone is here?" Everyone looked very unsure of what they could do. "Well, this sure is fun, let's stare at the wall opposite us in awkward silence! This isn't weird at all."

"Well, it didn't feel weird until you started complaining about it," Talia said. "Anyhow, I've got a game tomorrow, so I'll see you guys later."

"Okay then, and now they disperse..." Felicity said under her breath, flopping back on her pillow as she had sat up.

"I'm gonna go study," Carlos said, sitting up from the chair he had sat in for approximately 57.023 seconds. Carlos left with Talia and closed the door behind himself.

"Now they're gone, that wasn't a very long visit, was it? Are you two gonna leave? Then I'd be all alone," Felicity said, her arms hanging off the sides of the bed, but she started to get up.

"I guess not, I don't have anything I really need to do. I mean, isn't tomorrow the last day before spring break? I've already finished practically everything," Andrew said, shrugging.

"Well, I took a heavy load, and I have multiple things due by tomorrow night," Ingrid said, with her laptop on her lap. "Andrew, can I sit at the desk? It'd make life easier," she asked.

"Yeah, sure," Andrew said, getting up, and Ingrid took his seat. Felicity tossed the flicker at Andrew, but he smacked it up and fumbled it. Luckily he picked it up before anyone else could steal it and make a touchdown.

"Come on, sit over here and find us something to watch," Felicity said, tapping the end of the bed she wasn't sitting on. Andrew sat down and began to look for something.

CHAPTER vii

This one has a special place in my heart:

December was sitting on a bench. Ever since she had broken up with Carlos 3 months before, and had been very vocally cruel—not to mention how she punched him—things had been different with that group of friends.

Kira was in high school, and she was at college. 'Whoopie,' was her expression towards it, and it was more of a sarcastic type. The simplest way to put it was that December was miserable. She missed living with her family; she and Kira were close, and she missed her.

December always carried a gun on her, in case she decided to shoot Carlos, but that day she had left her Glock in her closet; she had forgotten to take it with her. This, in her mind, meant that she was finally getting over the whole ordeal, which felt depressing and good. Come to think of it, eating a donut felt depressing to her, walking in the sunshine was depressing, binge-watching whole TV shows was depressing, stubbing her toe was painful, and pain was depressing. Everything had a hint of depressingness.

It used to feel like she was against the world, but now it felt like the world was against her, and many of the occupants of the world were for her, and that confused her. She had never been much of a thinker, so she thought she should leave the thinking to others and not go to college, but when she left the thinking to others, they said she should go to college. In the end, she ended up sitting on a college bench.

She wondered if her biological mom was right. Was she really destined to live in a dumpster? Her old mom always said she'd live in a dumpster when she grew up. Was it really true? She felt like laying on the bench and going to sleep; she didn't really care about her own safety anymore. The problem was there was a bunch of darn mosquitos biting her, so she got up and began walking to her room.

December had no friends. She thought friends were for friends, and at the moment she wasn't anyone's friend, so she didn't have friends. As she walked, she ran into someone who looked lonely, which was an instant connection. "Hey," December said.

"Hello," the random guy in a black hoodie said.

"Well, no offense, but you sound lonely," December said, as she walked next to him. "What's your name? My name's December, like the month or something."

"You do too," he said, looking straight forward with his hoodie covering his face. "My name's Braden, and I don't normally talk this much to people."

December grabbed his hoodie's hood and pulled it down off his head. "Ohh, wow, you're pale. When's the last time your skin was in contact with the sun?" December asked, touching his very white, smooth skin. He had medium-long black hair that was a stark contrast with his skin.

"Now, seeing how the sun is still out. I don't need to be in the sun. I take supplements, so I'll be fine without it," he said, apparently not minding December touching his cheek and neck.

"That's another whole layer of depressing," December said, drawing her hand back, likely realizing she was being a weirdo. "Where are you going? Do you go to college here?" she asked, continuing to walk with him.

"I'm just walking through, which is to say I move a lot, so don't get used to my company." He still looked straight ahead as he walked. December stopped and he continued on his way. Instead of following, she went to her room. She lay down in her bed and started texting Kira, her younger sister. Even when she felt terrible, texting Kira made her happy. Kira always had that effect.

CHAPTER viii

Fine, I was lying, that wasn't dear to my heart:

"Puppy...puppy! Come here!" Kira was walking down a porch when she saw a previously white puppy come running up covered in mud. It jumped at her legs. "Dog, what's wrong with you? Get off me, you're disgusting, no, no!" The muddy puppy continued to try and jump on her. "Seriously, now I'm gross..." she groaned in irritation, then moved her leg at it, and it smacked its face into her leg at the same time. The puppy yelped and ran away a couple of feet, then lay down, staring at her.

"Ohh, fine, come here!" she said, tapping the porch she was now sitting on. "You're fine, get over here!" The fat little messy puppy started walking over, laying its head on her lap, and flopping down the rest of its body. She began to pet it, trying her best to only pet the mostly clean parts when her phone dinged. "Let me look at this real quick, pup," she said, pulling out her phone and seeing that December had texted.

December's text: "Hey, Kira, how's the puppy? I can't believe Dad finally got you one! What did you/are you gonna name him? And yeah, spring break's in two days, I think. I wish I could go over now, but apparently, I'm supposed to finish my assignments first, lol."

"Other than being a complete dirty disaster, it's fine, and still very sweet; I just wish it didn't have to roll in mud, but it's a puppy. I'm not sure what to name it, I thought we could do that together. What do you think we should name it?

"Have you talked to Carlos yet? You know they aren't ones to hold grudges like that. Well, Ingrid can hold a grudge, but we've been friends with them for years. You can't just ignore that they exist!" Kira sent, referring back to a text before that December had successfully ignored for three texts.

'I don't want to talk about that, do you seriously have to bring that up again, Kira?' December thought to herself, feeling like she was being cheated. She began typing again: "I plan to, I just haven't found the time yet. Why does it really matter to you anyway? It's not like they're my only friends." She pressed send, trying to think of other friends she had.

Kira rolled her eyes practically as she read, 'Yeah, right! How dumb do you think I am? Can't you understand that they're still your friends? If you just had the guts to apologize, this stupidity might be over.' She began to type while rubbing the puppy with one hand. "Ohh, sure...and why didn't you talk to them then? I don't believe you...other friends? Name them..." she pressed send, irritated with December.

December read the text, surprised that Kira had called her bluff. Kira used to assume she was being completely honest with the truth, but now she was more willing to call out her "sis." December wasn't sure how to respond, mostly because she knew Kira was right, but she didn't want to admit it. What was supposed to be a relaxing, fun conversation with Kira turned out to be a frustrating debate that she knew she was wrong in.

That's life.

CHAPTER ix
This is incredibly useful. Five stars:

"Bingo! Bingo! Bingo!" Zeus yelled in excitement. "I love bingo! Haha, I always win!" He took a pile of dollar bills and stuffed them in a bag.

"This is all luck, how do you always win? I'm done with this!" Duellona said, irritated that she couldn't win.

"The game is not completely based on luck but is highly influenced by chances. The reason why Zeus continues to beat us is because he is using methods that have been made to improve the likelihood of winning. It seems that the chances have not been favorable to me, as I also have used proper strategy without victory," Athena said, calm and soothing as always, sounding very profound as she spoke.

"I think bingo's pretty fun," Euphrosyne said, "but maybe we could play something like Life to mix it up."

"I hate Life," Duellona said, but nobody was really sure what she meant by "life," because there were three things she could likely be referring to: First, life as in living things; second, life as in her life that she was living; and third, the board game called *Life*. She explained herself as she noticed their blank stares, "I mean the game—it requires very little strategy, just like bingo."

"Let's play guts!" Euphrosyne yelled in excitement. "I used to play in the Navy, and we'd lose tons of money at a time!" Nobody else seemed to think losing tons of money at a time sounded terribly fun.

"How about we play Axis & Allies," Duellona suggested, and Athena seemed to be on board with it. Euphrosyne was easy to please and was willing to play any of the games they chose. Zeus, on the other hand, didn't really care for strategy games. "Okay, it's decided—we're playing it!" Duellona exclaimed, pulling it off a shelf.

"Wait, I hate Axis & Allies..." Zeus complained, but his protests went unnoticed. An hour later, the board was finally set up, and they were ready to play, although Euphrosyne still didn't really grasp the rules. "Well, at least let me be Athena's partner," Zeus said.

"Me and Duellona are the Axis; you and Rosyne are the Allies," Athena explained in her usual beautiful voice. They continued long into the night. Zeus felt that it was unfair, given their backgrounds in war, but he played nonetheless.

...Time passed, (as represented by those dots) it was morning, and Zeus dozily rolled his dice in a Hail Mary effort to destroy Germany; he succeeded, but the next round it was taken back...three hours passed by, and finally the Axis was on the brink of victory...

"Wait, the rules say a tank can only move two spaces, not three, and you can only make as many troops as this number right here," Euphrosyne said, pointing to what represented a factory on the board. "So, you technically couldn't have made that many tanks, and they couldn't have attacked us like they did ten rounds ago, but it's okay, I don't care."

"Yes, we do care! I'm not gonna lose just because they're a bunch of cheats! We've been playing too long to let that happen," Zeus said, trying to get back a chance to win the game he had lost a while ago.

"Those must be new rules, I've never played like that..." Duellona said, and the debate continued until they decided to make breakfast and forget about the game. The debate specifically ended when Athena and Duellona suggested they could start another game using the correct rules; Zeus at that point realized how little he wanted to play the game.

It was time to head to college and do what they had planned to do. Namely kill Carlos, Ingrid, Felicity, and possibly anyone that stood in their way. Zeus planned on using very powerful tasers, while the others were a little less refined.

"Urrrauuuuthhhhh...blehhh..." Felicity was throwing up in the bathroom; Ingrid and Andrew were very glad she wasn't doing it on the carpet but felt bad for her. "Are you alright in there?" Andrew asked and was returned with, "No...I feel awful..." and the muffled noise of Felicity throwing up again.

"Well, I guess this is a sleepover now; well, at least one of us has to stay with her," Andrew said, turning to Ingrid, who was just finishing up the final touches to an assignment. He sat on the bed, turning off a movie they were halfway through.

"Well, no offense, but I don't think it's very appropriate for just you to stay, and I'm not so sure if it's really allowed," Ingrid said, looking back from her computer. "I mean, I'll stay with her, and you can too if you want, but you don't have to; you've been with her for a while now."

"I know, I guess we'll both stay here then, and probably get no sleep, but that's alright," Andrew said, and went to knock on the bathroom door, which was unlocked, but Felicity wanted privacy while throwing up, so it was closed. The light reflecting off the door signaled through his eyes and to his brain that it was moving and thus being opened. His brain signaled to his hand to stand ready in case it for some reason still needed to knock.

Felicity walked out, but it was more of a drowsy stumble type of walk. "Are you sure that stuff you sprayed in her nose is doing its job?" Andrew asked, helping her to the bed.

"I may need to apply it again, but it's definitely the right thing to use." Ingrid, for some unknown reason, carried anti-opioid Narcan medicine with her.

"Where'd you even get that stuff? And why'd you have it just on you like that?" Andrew asked, leaning over to help Felicity.

"I have it because we're on a college campus; do you know how many people overdose at college? I'm surprised I haven't had to help anyone yet," Ingrid said, but Andrew thought it would have sounded more like Ingrid to not carry it simply because she despised people who would need it. But even Ingrid understood there was value in a person's life, even if that person was doing incredibly stupid things. "She couldn't have taken more than two tablets, or she'd be a lot worse off and would most definitely need to go to urgent care. I'm not sure if we should take her; what do you think?"

"Uhhh, I don't know about this stuff; won't it just go out of her system or something?" he asked, shrugging.

"Eventually, but it slows her breathing, and if it slows too much, well, she could altogether stop breathing. She's technically overdosed, not like we normally think of, but she took too much, and it exaggerates the normal side effects," Ingrid said, reasoning to herself in her answer to him. "That's why I gave her the naloxone; it blocks the receptors, which should start to stop the effects. Depending on how much she took, the effects should begin to fade—actually, they should start to fade pretty soon."

"You're making it sound like she's gonna be fine, but at the same time, it's possible that she might not be," Andrew said, thinking that Ingrid had already decided what they would do. Furthermore, he thought that Ingrid had decided not to take Felicity to any health or medical center.

"How can you stop breathing without dying? Or is somebody dying? This doesn't make any sense..." Felicity said, leaning against the wall as she sat on her bed.

Many hours passed by; most classes were completely finished, but a few students had classes. Ingrid, Andrew, and hopefully Felicity had all finished their assignments.

Andrew felt himself falling back for the seventh time. In response, he jerked awake and opened his eyes. Felicity was sleeping, and so was Ingrid. His neck was sore. He blinked his eyes awake as they adjusted to the faint light coming through the apartment's only window. He opened and closed his mouth, wondering where all the moisture had gone, and rubbed his tongue up against his teeth, thinking about brushing them. At least Felicity was feeling better and not dead.

He grabbed his keys and texted Ingrid that he was going to get them some breakfast, thinking she would see it when she woke up. Twenty minutes passed by. Ingrid was up and wondering when Andrew had left until she looked at her phone and saw what he had texted her. Ingrid heard the door open, and Andrew walked into the apartment carrying a paper bag full of food. Ingrid inwardly considered the effects of eating breakfast sandwiches, how the fat and grease caused plaque buildup inside her veins. The extremely large doses of salt, the obscene amounts of calories.

Ingrid lived steadfastly to a diet of her own devising, based on many studies she had read in her research. It consisted of many vegetables, certain breads, potatoes of all kinds, and occasionally very lean meats. In her diet, oil and dairy were banned, refined sugar was discouraged but permissible, and eggs were banned. Workouts were mandatory; stretching as part of her workout was also mandatory, and mental exercise was even more mandatory. Mental exercise being an obscene amount of study.

With all this in mind, Ingrid couldn't help but think whether or not she would have to eat a greasy biscuit to be polite. She did care about being polite after all.

Andrew knew of Ingrid's strange dieting habits and thus bought her a salad. Breakfast was short work. Felicity was soon up and began to eat. She looked rather tired or exhausted.

Zeus drove into the college campus and parked. Euphrosyne was dressed rather prettily, or more cutely, in a dress that looked like it belonged in Ancient Greece. She looked like she was 9-10 years old.

"What do we do now, Duellona?" Zeus asked, unwrapping a breakfast sandwich they had gotten on the way, at a gas station.

"I want to kill them so badly!" Euphrosyne said, doing a little skip. Athena, as always, stood with perfect posture. She now wore a rather shiny suit of armor with gold and things, and a sword at her side.

"We will find them. I believe Felicity lives in room 115, Carlos in room 43, and Ingrid in room 206," Duellona said, unstrapping a spear from the top of the car.

"That sounds like a lot of walking. Don't we have cars now so we don't have to walk? My knees are so bad; you can hear them crack," Zeus said, walking slowly away from the group.

"The apartments aren't over there; you're walking away from them," Athena said, raising an eyebrow.

"How do you know that I am not walking in the direction they are in, while you want to walk in the direction of their rooms?"

Andrew pulled his car up next to theirs and got out. "Woahhh, hold on guys, is there a comic event, or D&D? Are y'all enthusiasts too?" Euphrosyne looked clueless but happy, and Zeus began walking back towards Andrew.

"Yes, we are D&D enthusiasts and actors; we came for a show and a LARP-ing tournament," Athena seemed to have forgotten the enthusiast part of "enthusiast." Her voice contained very little expression or joy.

"Would you by chance know where a person named Fobee is, or Carlos, or possibly...what's her name... Fellahiky? We need to find them," Zeus asked, breakfast sandwich in hand.

"Yeah, I don't know those people. I know two different Carlos's, but they probably aren't the ones you're referring to; there are a lot of Carlos's, I think."

"Thanks, you're a real help..." Zeus said sarcastically, turning back to the others. "That's the problem with this generation; they don't even think when you ask them a question!"

"Uhhh, it was nice meeting you, but I have to go; have a good one." Andrew walked off towards the apartments, a bag in hand.

A few minutes passed when the group started walking towards the dorms, specifically to Ingrid's apartment.

Nobody was there, so they decided to go to Felicity's apartment. "Maybe they already left for spring break," Zeus proposed.

"That would make our lives harder," Duellona noted.

CHAPTER x

Not happened quite yet:

"I'm going to my room. You can do the same, Andrew - Felicity looks fine," Ingrid said, standing up and stretching.

"Why is Andrew going to your room? Oh, wait a second, I see, you meant that he should go to his room, right?" Felicity reasoned although she looked a little sleepy.

Both Ingrid and Andrew were soon gone, leaving Felicity eating a sandwich on her bed. There was a knock at the door and Felicity looked up, startled, wondering who it could be. The door began to creak open, and she heard a man's voice.

CHAPTER xi

Wasn't that intense? Wait until you see this part:

"What the heck? You can't just barge into my room, Derek! I'm probably getting changed, gosh! What's wrong with you?" Felicity yelled, realizing whose voice it was.

"Ohh, sorry, I was worried because you didn't answer my knock. Wait. Probably changing? What does that even mean?" He had the door just ever so slightly open, and Felicity shut it the rest of the way, locked it, and put the bolt lock into place.

"Felicity, what are you doing in there?" he asked.

"Locking the door so you can't come in! I already told you we're done; I don't want to talk to you. You make everything awkward!"

"What do you mean? This doesn't sound like you. A couple of days ago, I thought everything was great, but now you suddenly change! It doesn't make any sense." A couple of seconds passed by with no response from Felicity. "Let me in, babe, please! Just tell me what's wrong."

"Don't call me that; that's disgusting!" Felicity paused before continuing. "What's wrong is I don't want to date you or marry you! It just seemed hard to tell you I don't like you!"

"Can't we talk about this? Why can't you just open the door?" Derek asked.

"Excuse me, but why do you have your face up against the door like that?" Zeus asked, tapping Derek on the shoulder. "And is this by chance Feelicty's room?" Athena corrected him by saying, "Felicity."

"Uhhh, yeah, she's my girlfriend," Derek said.

"Not for long..." Euphrosyne giggled, but was overshadowed by Felicity yelling, "No, I'm not!"

Zeus scratched his head. "Relationship problems? In my experience, the girls want you if you act like you don't want them." Athena, Duellona, and Euphrosyne all raised their right eyebrows as if to say, "You sure? Because it's not working on us."

"Can you leave now? We want to talk to Felicity, and it seems like she hates you," Euphrosyne said, happy as always.

"Alright, you can shut your gob, or I'm warning you, I'm gonna lose it!" Derek said, pointing at Euphrosyne. In a flash, his finger was slashed off by her kukri. He screamed like a girl as he looked in shock at his hand. His shock was soon turned quite literal by Zeus; Euphrosyne giggled at what she'd done.

"What's happening out there, Derek?" Felicity asked a worried tone in her voice. All she heard from Derek was a muffled "run," which seemed rather silly as she was in a dorm room. "Thud!" sounded off the door, scaring Felicity.

"What are you doing!?" Felicity yelled.

"Trying to kill you!" Euphrosyne yelled back, and Zeus complained, "You're not supposed to tell her that!"

Felicity looked to her window, and in five seconds she was running down the emergency fire escape. When she reached the ground, she looked around, heart pounding like a fat guy on a treadmill. Without any real thought, she started off running across the campus, passing a random guy mowing.

She looked back, and nobody was behind her. Her running was brought to an abrupt stop, or rather a flying stop as she tripped over the body of a figure looking at a beetle. Felicity let out a scream (something becoming common for her) and landed with a squeak mixed with a groan.

The figure re-balanced himself and looked at Felicity. Dressed in all black, he was the same Braden December had met the night before. He mumbled something, then said, "That was inconsiderate, wasn't it?" With no response from Felicity, he continued studying his beetle.

Felicity began getting up, looking at her arms that now had scratches across them. Her attention was then brought to the beetle-studying man. "Uhh, who are you? What's happening?"

"I am the one you just tripped over. You should watch where you run," he said slowly, thoughtful depression filtering in through his words.

"I tripped over you?" Felicity asked, blushing, "I um, I didn't mean to."

"Yes, yes of course," he said, poking a stick at his beetle. With a sudden motion, he lifted his head, looked at the way Felicity had come from, and then at Felicity. "Who were you running from? You seem scared," he said, slowly.

Felicity jerked as if let out of a trance; her eyes began darting everywhere at once as she checked her surroundings. "You need to call the police!" She gasped, trying to breathe.

"No use," he said, "The police would only arrest me, they tend to not be fond of me," he mumbled something more, but it was unintelligible. Beginning to stand up he said, "Come along now, we need to have a conversation."

Felicity stood up a little dizzy, "You're not gonna do anything? But, but...Derek's...they'll kill him!" She pleaded, looking like she was about to run back to where she left Derek.

"No, they won't," he said casually.

"How do you know that?" Felicity asked, almost accusingly.

"He's already dead, they can't kill a dead person," he explained.

"What! No! You...you...can't know...you can't say that!"

"Hmmm, you could look at his corpse, if that would console you."

"What is wrong with you?! He's not dead! He's fine!"

"He is dead, but...we can go back to the room if you desire. Braden."

"What? His name is Derek!"

"My name is Braden, spelled B R A D E N, and no, I don't care what your name is."

"My name's Felicity."

"Hmmm, as if when you trip and conquer a city at the same time," Braden reflected.

With that, Felicity dragged Braden along. As they walked, Felicity told him he should call the police, and he eventually gave in, but they found that the police were already there.

"Jerry, he is dead, isn't he?" Braden yelled at a police officer.

"I can't disclose that information to you at the moment," the officer responded.

"What do you mean!? He's my boyfriend, let me see him!" Felicity had a tendency to yell a lot, it seems.

"Hmmm," the officer thought, technically he could talk to her, but Braden was greatly disliked and distrusted by the police. "I'm afraid to say there was nothing we could do when we found him, miss," he said solemnly.

"Sounds about right," Braden commented.

Felicity began to get all teary and blubber, thinking about all the many things she did wrong because she was generally a failure of a friend to Derek right before he died. Obviously, her crying would accomplish nothing and was completely futile, but she did it anyway.

"Can we go now? Who knows who else they plan to murder?" Braden half complained.

Felicity looked like a minions GIF as she said, "Whaaaaat?" through her tears.

CHAPTER xii

Back to Ingrid:

Ingrid looked like an astonished piglet as she walked up to her room. The door was wide open, her room was a disaster, and there was a half-eaten breakfast sandwich on her desk.

"If this is a prank..." her words trailed off as she looked around her room, finding there was nobody else in it. This reminded her of squatter activity, and not the type you see at the gym, although you'd think old gyms would be a prime target for all kinds of squatters.

Her mind snapped back into normal Ingrid supercomputer mode. Pulling out her phone, she texted Andrew, Carlos, Talia, Felicity, and technically December, but December hadn't responded to anything in quite a while.

"Somebody was in my room; please tell me why."

From a different perspective:

"We are gathered here today, for the sake of our beloved Murphy. He passed this morning in the whistling of the birds he so furiously hated. After being hit with an electric dart, weighing a whole quarter pound, he never recovered. Oddly enough, he helped in the saving of the one that so afflicted him.

It was that day that the whole campus heard rumors of a murder, and Murphy saw a strange group of people dressed as gods of old fleeing the scene of the crime. He immediately went without fear to the crime scene where he soon met a blubbering girl and a sad man, but that sad man he had talked to before. It was none other than Braden, although his real name is Orcus.

Murphy told Braden of his findings, and Braden followed in pursuit of the criminals. The blubbering girl followed Braden in hopes of exacting revenge on the murders. When they tracked down Zeus and the others, they found Ingrid, Andrew, and Carlos running like girls.

Murphy bravely threw a nut directly into the left eye of Duellona. The blubbering girl pulled out a Glock she'd pickpocketed from the officer, who was technically a detective and had the gun in a much too big holster. She began shooting like a madwoman. According to Murphy, she missed every time, so he took the gun to finish them, but the earth under the "gods" began to fall and quickly consumed them. It is said that Orcus/Braden stood on the edge of the great pit and saluted Murphy before he stepped back into it, at which point it closed over them.

Murphy saved the one named Carlos, even though Carlos caused Murphy pain and suffering. Murphy was such a role model for any squirrel, but ultimately he succumbed to a mental illness. After biting a woman in the thigh, it is believed he contracted rabies. He died at 3 am, scratching unknown, yet surely wise, writings in the hollow of the tree he called home," an old, graying squirrel said, trying to regain his breath after giving such a long speech.

Around the speaker, there were gathered many squirrels, all waiting to get a part of Murphy's old belongings. Two carried out his body and chucked him out of the tree; a hawk caught him before he hit the ground. Murphy screamed in fright, "I'm not dead! Ahhh! Murdererrrrsssss!"

All the squirrels gasped, and an albino squirrel said, "Oop, my bad, he looked pretty dead to me, honestly my mistake."

"Well, he's dead now, so we can continue the auction," the old gray squirrel said. Thus they continued the auction.

Revisiting the scene explained above from a more neutral perspective:

"Ola!" Murphy yelled at Braden as Felicity blubbered like a baby that had stubbed its pinky toe. "Brotha! There are some weirdos chasing that kid who shot me! They'll kill him before I get the chance if you don't stop them!"

Braden looked up from his thoughts as he heard Murphy. Apparently, he was the only one hearing what Murphy was saying. He whispered something to Felicity, at which point she scrubbed her eyes and looked up at him. In a sudden movement, she hugged the officer, who let out a bit of air in a gasping manner.

The two, that is, Felicity and Braden, went running off a second later, leaving the officer feeling really weird, but lunch was really at the top of Officer Jerry's mind. Felicity wasn't sure what she was doing, but she ran along with Braden, tucking away the gun she had stolen from the officer. In no time, they caught a glimpse of the four panting 'gods,' and Felicity's friends running helter-skelter.

When they finally arrived at where the gods were, everyone goosed... sorry... ducked as Felicity shot the pistol she had stolen from Jerry. Zeus screamed in pain as he clutched his knees, "Ahhhh! My arthritis is flaring up, somebody help me!"

The three goddesses all raised their right eyebrows as they felt the earth rumble under them and saw the shooter and Braden. Zeus rolled in pain and tears, "Ohhh, why did I try to run after them? My joints...the pain!"

Duellona stumbled back as an acorn hit her in the eye, and Murphy jumped on Felicity so that she fell back and dropped her gun. Murphy grabbed it and started dragging it over to where Carlos was staring blankly at the strange scene. Ingrid turned back, looking at what was happening. Andrew attempted to turn back but slipped and ate dirt.

The earth began collapsing under the four gods, then gave way forming a pit that they fell into. Braden walked over to the hole and said,

"Peace out! Say bye to December for me!" at which point he stepped back and fell into the pit which began closing after him.

CHAPTER xiii

P*AUSE!*
You likely read the last scene and are acutely unaware of what has happened. Don't worry, it is common for the human race to fail at easy tasks. But being a kind person I shall give you a briefly extended summary of what has happened.

Derek went to visit Felicity, as you know, but he found she was quite hostile, and would not let him in the room. The four gods then also arrived and assaulted Derek. As Felicity heard his screams, she ran or climbed out of the window. Not knowing she had escaped, the gods attempted to bust the dorm room's door open at which they found she was gone.

Ingrid, finding her room ransacked, texted their group chat at which Carlos and Andrew came to her room. But hearing a commotion, they decided to check up on Felicity. When they arrived, they found Felicity's room was also ransacked, and Derek was dead. At once they called the police but then heard a commotion going on outside. They ran and found the gods were attempting to make an escape, finding it immediately suspicious, and seeing blood dripping from Euphrosyne's blade, they attempted to make chase.

The gods at this point recognized Carlos and Ingrid as their targets. At which the pursuers (Carlos, Ingrid, and Andrew) became the pursued. Realizing they had four murderous maniacs on their tails made them run like they also were lunatics.

Felicity, as you well know, ran into Braden as she fled. After a bit of discussion, they went to visit the scene of Derek's demise. Felicity was hoping she could help Derek if he was still alive. When they arrived, the police were already at the scene. Braden (who is not all he seems as seen in summoning a hole into the depths of the earth, but you probably forgot he did that) whispered to Felicity that the ones who had murdered Derek were in a certain direction. Felicity rubbed her eyes from tears and spontaneously hugged the police officer, stealing his firearm.

Braden and Felicity at once ran off, becoming the pursuers of the pursuers. When they caught up to the gods, Felicity began shooting like a wild cowgirl and the gods hopped and flopped in fright. Zeus specifically fell to the ground clutching his knees because of his severe arthritis, practically ignoring the gunfire.

Braden caused a pit to form under the gods, the earth shook a bit as it crumbled under them, and they fell in terror. Braden walked over to the hole or tomb that he had made and essentially said, "Peace out," then let himself free fall into the pit. It is speculated Braden is/was the god of death, sometimes called Orcus. Thus the hole into the earth was simply a path into the underworld. (See image for an explanation of "Underworld.")

Murphy the squirrel is also in the past scenes, but I trust you to pay attention to what is written and remember the role that he has played.

With that as the summary, we will go back into the thick of the scene we interrupted to fit this in. (End of summary going into the scene now.)

The ground formed back into a little crater with four black marble-like stones and one white one in the center. They were on a dying fire in the crater and had writing on them. Felicity got up from her fright and kicked Murphy like a football as he was still trying to drag the pistol to shoot Carlos. Murphy tumbled across the ground, then gave Felicity the evil stare before climbing up into a tree.

Carlos went over to Felicity, Andrew stood up with his nose bleeding, and Ingrid inspected the crater completely speechless. Felicity grabbed the pistol off the ground, hiding it away in her clothes.

As you may guess, other college students began coming, wondering what was causing such a disturbance. Ingrid's eyes locked on the little fire and five marble-like stones. She promptly tapped them with her foot, to which the fire responded by dying. Noticing that people were coming, she picked them up with her hoodie sleeve and put them in her hoodie's pocket.

As the police began to arrive, they found there was a large crowd of students, doing nothing but whispering very loudly. The group began to steal away before the police could establish any order. December, being a student attracted by all the fuss, was in the crowd. When she saw Felicity, Ingrid, Carlos, and Andrew all together, she instinctively ran over to them, knowing they must have had something to do with what was happening. She also knew something was up because of the group text she had read.

They were surprised to see December, while at the same time, she did have a habit of showing up at weird times. Contrary to what you may assume, their walking away from the scene wasn't really suspicious, as many college students were doing the same. Mostly because nobody wanted to be made out as a witness or have to be questioned by the police.

Once they had gotten pretty far away, December asked what was going on. Felicity said what she knew, which wasn't much. Nobody really knew what was happening. Ingrid pulled out the stones she had grabbed and showed them to everyone in the group. They decided to meet Talia at the library. She had had a soccer game, but it was suddenly canceled because of all that had happened.

They sat down at a table in the library. Ingrid explained how she grabbed them, then picked up one with her bare hand. (Before she had only touched them with her hoodie sleeve pulled up over her hand.) Fiery letters scrolled across the little stone, it read "Athena, goddess of wisdom," which she read out loud.

Intrigued, the rest of the group each grabbed one, except Andrew. December grabbed the white one, which said, "Orcus, god of death." Carlos looked at his and it said, "Zeus, god of Lightning." Felicity's said, "Euphrosyne goddess of joy," and Talia's said, "Duelona, goddess of war."

Andrew asked, "So, what are these things again? And, why are they all really old gods?"

"I don't know, but they're pretty cool looking!" Felicity said.

"Um, guys..." Carlos said, seeing electricity hopping between his fingers.

Ingrid then explained: "These small stones contain the power of the god written on them. The person who first touches the stone will receive the power, almost in a demi-god sort of way. There are many benefits to owning one of these, such as extended life, a form of special gift or ability dependent on what god's stone you have, and many other things. There are two ways these stones can appear, white and black. A white stone is that of a living god, and a black stone is that of a dead god. White stones were often given to a god's right-hand man so that they became a sort of demigod." Ingrid blinked as she finished speaking, then said, "Wait, what just happened?"

"Why does that not sound good?" Andrew asked.

"The only white stone is the god of death, that's ironic," December said.

Thus they became, in a sense, superhumans, except Andrew. Although Felicity was a rather cheery person, she made sure to share some of that with him. December reconciled with her friends once more. They were the only people she knew with superhuman powers, after all. It shouldn't be said that it wasn't awkward at first... it was, but Carlos forgave rather easily as a habit. (Carlos and December had a form of...disagreement...which led to a sucker punch to Carlos' guts, nose, and oddly enough December pinched his cheek really hard, most likely the worst of all three.)

Derek was dead, and as is the habit of dead people, he was to be buried. His funeral was held a week after his death, which they all went to. Derek was an exceptional person and student, his loss struck them like an iron brick a day or two after his death, and freshly at the funeral.

They were all on break, so December got to go back to her lovely and annoying little sister. Kira was actually a great sister, she lived with December as a sister, so she'd have to be pretty remarkable.

The puppy! Please say you didn't forget that gorgeous little fellow? Well, December and Kira chose a name, and that name is... I'm sorry in advance... They named him Kevin. Almost cute if he didn't sound like that random business owner across the street.

Felicity and Andrew became buddies. I'd tell you all about romantic date nights at the local burger joint, but stuffing their faces really wasn't that interesting to watch. But, hey, it worked out for them in the end.

Talia played soccer, it was her battlefield, and if you decided you wanted to play her, you got your butt whupped. If you wanted to hear about romantic gooshies in this department, you looked in the wrong place. She probably eventually found some guy named Steve, but you will have to imagine what happened there.

Carlos broke everyone's expectations by becoming a DJ, and an epic one too. College didn't do much for him, except that lightning fingers were an awesome party trick. You may wonder what their "Super powers" did for them, and it didn't actually affect them that much for a while. But they were going to live longer than an average human, which eventually led to them learning more about the powers they possessed. Shall we just say, it didn't end well for everyone? (But that took about 70-100 years, so stop crying about it. Andrew not having special powers died within 70 years, so it didn't end great for him.)

Thus our story comes to a close.

THE LOUSY END

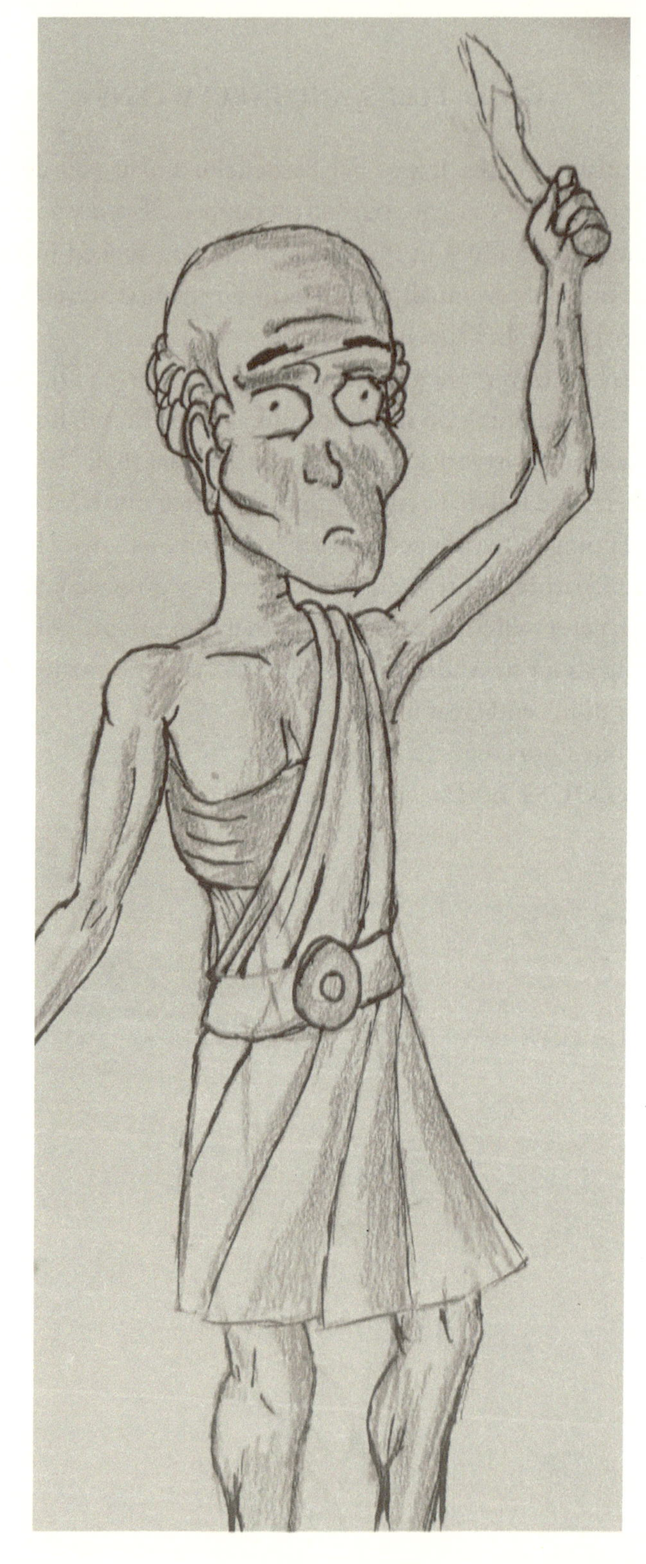

Don't miss out!

Visit the website below and you can sign up to receive emails whenever Colin Davidson publishes a new book. There's no charge and no obligation.

https://books2read.com/r/B-A-LYWPC-ALNDF

BOOKS 2 READ

Connecting independent readers to independent writers.

Did you love *Gods, Teens, and Inbetweens*? Then you should read *Cars, Computers, and Chaos*[1] by Travis Cramer!

[2]

Step into the world of Adrian, Erica, Scott, and Phoebe. A world filled with "Misadventure and Mystery" where deception and crime seems to lurk at every corner. Join the four of them as they work together to take down hackers, car thieves, and stalkers.

Erica, always the hotheaded one, is determined to bring these people to justice. Scott, creative and chaotic as he is, often holds the group together when things get rough. Phoebe might be a nerd, and a dedicated one at that, but don't underestimate her ability to solve a problem once she gets going! And Adrian, with his keen wit and sensible ideas might just be the person they need to solve the case.

---

1. https://books2read.com/u/mgykoz

2. https://books2read.com/u/mgykoz

As you read this book, prepare to be asking yourself burning questions, such as, "Are all the crimes connected?" or, "Are our heroes in over their heads?" Have no fear, these questions will be answered when you dive into the first book of the "Misadventure and Mystery" series, "Cars, Computers, and Chaos!"

Read more at https://books2read.com/ap/81Do3O/ Travis-Cramer.

About the Author

After I was born the, doctors had some stuff to say; there was a strange void in my brain. Some said it was a worm-hole, some said it was a small galaxy, others said it was the remarkable concept of nothing in real life.

Not to brag, but my mom always said I was special, so did the doctors, and really everyone in my life, now that I think about it. I've always known I must do something with my gift, so one day I started writing, and I kept writing, and now I'm an author, so cheers!

About the Publisher

Travis Cramer is a 17-year-old publishing whiz (yes, definitely) living in Delaware, though he once called New Jersey home (he's still not over leaving the pizza behind). Armed with a computer and a keyboard and way too many random ideas, Travis is a creative force who's always got a project up his sleeve. Whether he's editing stories, coming up with wacky new concepts, or convincing his friends that Delaware is cooler than it seems, Travis is making waves in the publishing world. He's basically a mad scientist of words, ready to take the world by storm—one typo at a time.